The Guyanese Princess

SHAJADA SIMON

Order this book online at www.trafford.com
or email orders@trafford.com

Most Trafford titles are also available at major online book retailers.

Trafford
PUBLISHING® www.trafford.com
North America & international
toll-free: 844 688 6899 (USA & Canada)
fax: 812 355 4082

Our mission is to efficiently provide the world's finest, most comprehensive book publishing
service, enabling every author to experience success. To find out how to publish your
book, your way, and have it available worldwide, visit us online at www.trafford.com

ISBN: 978-1-6987-0663-4 (sc)
ISBN: 978-1-6987-0662-7 (e)

Library of Congress Control Number: 2021906085

Print information available on the last page.

Trafford rev. 04/23/2021

The Guyanese Princess

By: Shajada Simon

Kya is a poor girl with big dreams of being a princess. Not knowing her father and his background story, he wants to meet her. But Kya is very hesitant about meeting her father. She has a very terrible image of him but tries to be happy just to please her grandmother. When she finally meets him she's in for a big surprise.

There once was a teenage girl who came from a poor family. Her name was Kya. She had a big dream of being a young BEAUTIFUL princess. However, she doubted that a girl like her becoming a princess was highly unlikely to happen. She lived in Queenstown, in the county of Essequibo, Guyana, a small country in South America, with her mother, grandmother, sister, and brothers. She never had a vivid image of her father, since he left when she was 5 years old. He never called or came to visit, but the one thing she didn't know is he was royalty.

Map of Guyana

Victoria Regia lily

National Bird
canje pheasant
(Hoatzin)

One day, Kya heard her mom yelling and crying but she didn't know why. So she asked, "Mom what is going on?" Her mom couldn't look at her. She was embarrassed and didn't want her daughter to see her like that. The phone was still on and Kya heard a voice, so she answered "Hello who is this? I am Kya."

"Hello Kya, I am Ranuel." In a nervous tone, he quickly hung up on her. His voice sounded very familiar even though she never saw him. Kya wondered why he hung up on her. After all, she did nothing wrong. But at that point she didn't care. She wanted to know who was that man and what he did to her mom. Kya slowly lifted her mom head and asked, "Who is Ranuel?"

Kya's mom looked up. "That was your father" her mom said sadly. Kya couldn't believe it. She had never talked to or seen her father. But she started to wonder why he hung up on her if he knew it was her . Kya started to think and wonder but she couldn't figure it out. Her mom saw that she was about to cry so she hugged her and the tears started to flow.

The next day Kya woke up sad but determined to find out why her dad hung up on her. Kya walked into the living room where her mother and grandmother sat. "Grandma I have something to ask you." "Yes sweetheart you can ask me," her grandma replied. So Kya took a deep breath and told her grandma everything she recently experienced about her dad. Her grandmother was shocked but felt bad for her granddaughter. But there was something very important she had to tell her grandchildren.

Grandma called all the kids to the living room including Kya's younger sister and 2 brothers. "Grandma" they all said in a curious tone. "What do you have to tell us? "There is something very important I have to tell you," responded their grandmother. When they heard that they knew it was something major. "Your father wants to see you. He wants you to see his home." They all became sad and Kya was very angry. "I am NOT going to his house after what he did to us. Are u CRAZY ?" she shouted and stormed out of the room before her grandmother could respond.

Kya grandmother quickly followed her."Kya, honey I know you're not making this easy, but you have to go," her grandmother said. "But grandma it's not right that we should visit him. I am 15 years old and I DON'T want to see him, " Kya shouted. After much persuasion from her grandmother, she reluctantly agreed to go visit her father. "Grandma, I am only doing it to make you happy," she said.

The next day they all got ready to see their father. Her mom and grandmother went along with them. He lived in Goed Fortuin, in the county Demerara, Guyana. It was a long-distance from Queenstown to Goed Fortuin. The had to take a 30 minutes trip by bus from Queenstown to Supenaam. From Supernaam, they had to take a 90 minutes ferry ride to Parika. They took a 45 minutes ride by bus from Parika to Goed Fortuin. The closer they were the more nervous Kya got. When they finally reached the house, was a mansion many times bigger than Kya's home. Kya went up to the door and rang the bell. "I am Kya your daughter," she said through the microphone. She heard the door open and saw his face. "I miss you honey," he said.

"Dad it's really you," Kya said nervously. It was her *dad* she was so shocked she didn't know how to react. "You all may come in," when they stepped into the house their jaws dropped. They couldn't believe how big the house was, the walls were freshly painted, everything looked nice and clean, and the six bedrooms were huge. Kya couldn't believe it. But why didn't my father insist that we lived with him, she questioned.

"Make yourself comfortable, you'll be living here," Ranuel said happily. Kya's siblings were happy so were her grandma and mother. Kya wasn't happy because she didn't feel right about living in the house. However, she kept quiet because she didn't want to ruin the happiness of her siblings. In her father's mansion, Each child including Kya would have their bedroom.Their bedrooms were huge and having lots of new clothes felt like a dream.

The first two days in her "New House" was cool but awkward. Kya didn't know how to act with her father. Kya avoided talking to her father because she didn't feel ready to get close to her him or to forgive him. So she stayed in her room a lot but knew she would have to come out soon.

Two weeks had past and Kya still hasn't spoken to her father, but today she finally went to talk to him. She knocked on his door "Father can I talk to you please" she said in a quiet tone "Yes honey" he said happily "Dad why did you leave for 10 years and now you want us back in your life?" Immediately Ranuel mood changed and he got emotional. "After I found out your mother was pregnant, I left because I was young and scared. We were just teens and breaking the news to my family would've caused many problems," Ranuel said sadly. Kya now knew why her father left, it was because of fear and disappointment.

The days felt different after her father told her the truth. She learned that he didn't leave because he wanted to but because of the pressures from his family members. Kya got closer to her father after years of absence. It felt like everything was a dream.

On one sunny day Ranuel called for everyone to come down for dinner that grandma had made. At the moment everyone was happy and Ranuel had even better news that would make Kya overly excited. "There is some exciting news I have to tell everyone," Kya and her family looked very confused. "I am a KING!!!!" That makes my two daughters princesses and my two sons,princes. Kya was most excited because that was her dream and it came true, the poor shy girl was now a princess.

The days that went by were happy and lovely for Kya .Kya was feeling like she was in heaven. She couldn't wait for the parade that the King had planned to welcome them home.

Kya prepared for that day to come. That she even practiced her princess wave in the mirror. She couldn't wait to see her dress. So all day she kept waving and smiling, later that day her mom called her down "Honey your dress is here." When Kya heard that she ran down the stairs so fast that she almost fell. The dress was beautiful. It was gold and sparkly and brought tears to her mom and grandma to tears. She couldn't wait for her dad to see her.

Today was the most important day in Kya's life. Everyone in the family looked wonderful. Her siblings wore green to represent the land, her mom and grandma wore blue to represent water and Kya and her father wore gold to represent royalty, love and courage. "Darling you look like the true princess you are," Ranuel said to Kya, she gave him a big hug and kiss.

They finally went on the parade and it was crazy. Everyone was screaming and applauding. Kya saw this woman and man hugging her father. So, she approached them and her father said "these are my parents." Kya was very scared because he didn't know how her grandparents would react to her. "Hello Kya, I am Mary your grandmother and this is your grandfather Lance, it's so wonderful to see you for the first time you're so beautiful." Her grandmother said. Kya felt so relieved "I'm happy to have you as my grandparents," she said as they gave each other big hugs. The day went great for Kya as she enjoyed the parade and the events that took place later on.

The new life Kya had was everything she wanted. She got to reunite with her father and build up memories that they missed. Her life as a princess is wonderful but she never forgot where she came from.

Printed in the United States
by Baker & Taylor Publisher Services